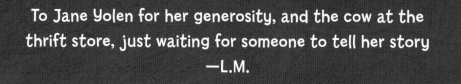

To Jane Yolen for her generosity, and the cow at the
thrift store, just waiting for someone to tell her story
—L.M.

For my fantastic agent, Rubin
—J.M.

Cindy Moo

Text copyright © 2012 by Lori Mortensen

Illustrations copyright © 2012 by Jeff Mack

All rights reserved. Manufactured in China.

No part of this book may be used or reproduced in any manner whatsoever without
written permission except in the case of brief quotations embodied in critical articles
and reviews. For information address HarperCollins Children's Books, a division of
HarperCollins Publishers, 10 East 53rd Street, New York, NY 10022.
www.harpercollinschildrens.com

Library of Congress Cataloging-in-Publication Data is available.
ISBN 978-0-06-204393-1

Typography by Rachel Zegar

12 13 14 15 16 S C P 10 9 8 7 6 5 4 3 2 1

❖

First Edition

Cindy Moo

By **Lori Mortensen**

Illustrated by **Jeff Mack**

HARPER

An Imprint of HarperCollinsPublishers

"Hey Diddle Diddle, the cat and the fiddle
The cow jumped over the moon.
The little dog laughed to see such sport
And the dish ran away with the spoon."

Over at the Diddle farm
a little bit past eight,
the cows all heard a nursery rhyme
that caused a great debate.

Diddle cows stood in the barn
and listened to each word
about the cow that jumped the moon,
amazed at what they heard.

"Across the moon?" cried Buttercup.

"No way!" said Honey Bun.
"The moon's too high and much too far.
It simply can't be done."

And as the cows scoffed at the thought,
a voice rose loud and true.

"Why can't a cow jump to the moon?"

That voice was Cindy Moo's.

The cows began to argue.
Each took a different side.
But in the end they all confessed
that none of *them* had tried.

So Cindy Moo raised up a hoof
and said that it was true.
"If *that* cow could jump the moon,
by golly, I can too."

As Cindy Moo waltzed to the field,
the others gathered 'round.
She'd jump that moon with room to spare
in one grand bovine bound!

She pawed her hooves.
She shook her head.

She ran and picked up speed.

And with a mighty MOO she jumped . . .

. . . across a prickly weed.

"Told you so," said Honey Bun.
"Too bad," said Buttercup.
"Cows weren't meant to jump the moon.
Why don't you just give up?"

But Cindy Moo ignored her friends.
She'd made a solemn vow.
She'd jump across the silver moon—
as soon as she knew how.

The next night after grazing,
she caught a stunning sight.
The moon was perched upon the hill,
a ball of silver light.

Cindy Moo let out a SNORT
and charged up to the top.
But when she reached the grassy peak,
she skidded to a . . .

stop!

Instead of staying on the hill—
much to her surprise—
the moon flew off the grassy ridge
back up to star-filled skies.

Cindy Moo plopped on the ground.
Would it be for naught?
"Jumping to the moon," she said,
"is harder than I thought."

Back inside the barn that night,
the worst of all came true.
Rain clouds swept the moon away—
now what was she to do?

She couldn't jump what wasn't there.
Perhaps the herd was right.
The moon and cows would never mix.
Not then, or any night.

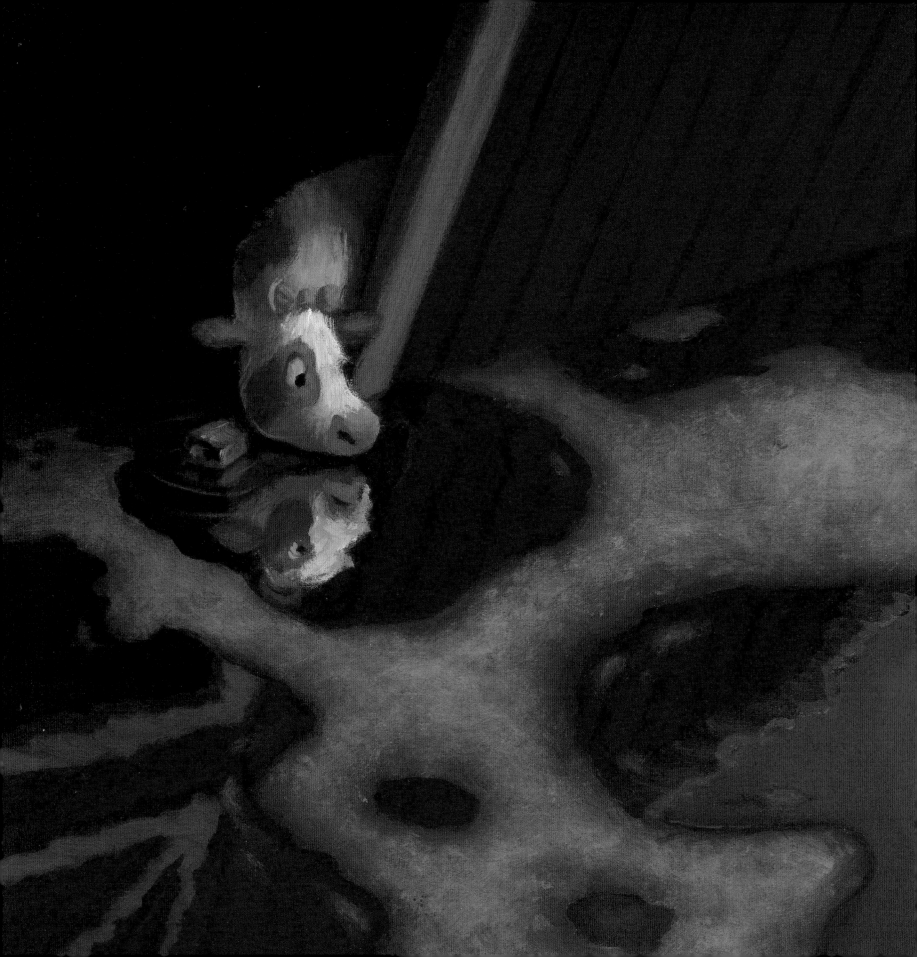

But late that night when raindrops stopped,
she peeked outside and found
the moon had slipped down to the earth
upon the rain-soaked ground.

Cindy Moo kicked up her heels

and raced with all her might.

And with a happy MOO she jumped . . .

Her friends came out and marveled much.
"Ms. Moo, you've done it now!"

"A cow *can* really jump the moon, as long as she knows how."

And ever since that rainy night,
the cows do not debate.
Whenever rain clouds pass their way
and it is growing late,
they gaze upon that puddled moon
and jump it two by two.
And guess who leads the Diddle herd?

Of course, it's Cindy Moo!